THE TINDER-BOX AND OTHER FAIRY TALES

HANS CHRISTIAN ANDERSEN

THE TINDER-BOX
AND OTHER
FAIRY TALES

Translated from the original Danish text

by R. P. Keigwin

Illustrations by Vilhelm Pedersen

HØST & SØN

THE TINDER-BOX AND OTHER FAIRY TALES

Copyright © 1989 & 2003 by Høst & Søn, Copenhagen

3. edition 2007

Cover by Ida Balslev-Olesen

The illustration on the cover is by Vilhelm Pedersen

Paper-cuttings by Hans Christian Andersen according to aggrement
with Odense City Museums

Typography: Dorte Cappelen

Printed in Denmark by Special-Trykkeriet Viborg a-s, Viborg 2007

ISBN 978-87-14-22023-5

I denne serie foreligger eventyr af H.C. Andersen på dansk, engelsk, fransk, hollandsk, ita-liensk, kinesisk, russisk, spansk, svensk og tysk. Udvalgene består af: **Dansk:** Klods-Hans, Kejserens nye klæder, Fyrtøjet, Den standhaftige tinsoldat, Svinedrengen, Tommelise, Den flyvende kuffert, Kærestefolkene, Den uartige dreng. **Engelsk:** Fyrtøjet, Stoppenålen, Den standhaftige tinsoldat, Hyrdinden og skorstensfejeren, Svinedrengen, Det er ganske vist!, Tommelise, Klods-Hans, Kærestefolkene. **Fransk:** Fyrtøjet, Lille Claus og store Claus, Den lille Idas blomster, Tommelise, Den uartige dreng, Kejserens nye klæder, Den standhaftige tinsoldat. **Hollandsk:** Klods-Hans, Stoppenålen, Fyrtøjet, Den standhaftige tinsoldat, Svinedrengen, Tommelise, Den flyvende kuffert, Kærestefolkene. **Italiensk:** Fyrtøjet, Stoppenålen, Den standhaftige tinsoldat, Hyrdinden og skorstensfejeren, Svinedrengen, Det er ganske vist!, Tommelise, Klods-Hans, Kærestefolkene. **Kinesisk:** Den grimme æl-ling, Tommelise, Den lille havfrue, Kejserens nye klæder, Nattergalen, Den lille pige med svovlstikkerne **Russisk:** Kejserens nye klæder, Snedronningen, Den grimme ælling, Prin-sessen på ærten, Stoppenålen. **Spansk:** Fyrtøjet, Prinsessen på ærten, Kejserens nye klæder, Den standhaftige tinsoldat, Svinedrengen, Den grimme ælling, Hyrdinden og skorstens-fejeren, Kærestefolkene, Den lille pige med svovlstikkerne. **Svensk:** Kejserens nye klæder, Den grimme ælling, Fyrtøjet, Klods-Hans, Svinedrengen, Den standhaftige tinsoldat, Grantræet. **Tysk:** Fyrtøjet, Stoppenålen, Den standhaftige tinsoldat, Hyrdinden og skor-stensfejeren, Svinedrengen, Det er ganske vist!, Tommelise, Klods-Hans, Kærestefolkene.

HØST & SØN · KØBMAGERGADE 62 · 1150 KØBENHAVN K

www.hoest.dk

CONTENTS

THE TINDER-BOX

Left, right! Left right!... Down the countryroad came a soldier marching. Left, right! Left, right!... He had his knapsack on his back and a sword at his side, for he had been at the war, and now he was on his way home. But then he met an old witch on the road. Oh! she was ugly – her lower lip hung right down on her chest. "Good evening, soldier," she said, "what a nice sword you've got, and what a big knapsack! You're a proper soldier! Now I'll show you how to get as much money as you want!" "Thank you very much, old dame!" said the soldier.

"Do you see that big tree over there?" said the witch, pointing to a tree near by. "It's quite hollow inside. Now, you must climb right up it, and then you'll see a hole; slip through this, and you'll come deep down into the tree. I will tie a rope round your waist, so that I can haul you up again, as soon as you give me a shout."

"But what am I to do down in the tree?" asked the soldier.

"Fetch money!" answered the witch. "For, mind you, when

you get down to the bottom of the tree, you will find yourself in a large passage. It's quite light there, because hundreds of lamps are burning there. Next, you will see three doors; you can open them all right, for the key's in the lock. If you go into the first room, you will see in the middle of the floor a big chest, with a dog sitting on it which has got eyes as big as tea-cups; but never you mind about that! I'll give you my blue-check apron, and you can spread it out on the floor. Then go along quickly and lift off the dog and put it on my apron; open the lid of the chest and take just as many pennies as you like. They are all copper, but if you would rather have silver, then you must go into the next room. There sits a dog with eyes as large as mill-wheels, but never you mind about that! Put the dog down on my apron, and help yourself to the money! And yet, if it's gold you want, you can get that too – as much as ever you can carry – if only you go into the third room. But this time the dog which is sitting on the money-chest has two eyes each one as big as the Round Tower... Something like a dog, I can tell you! But never you mind a bit about that! Just put the dog down on my apron, and then it won't do you any harm, and you can take as much gold out of the chest as you like."

"That doesn't sound at all bad," said the soldier. "But tell me, old witch, what am I to give you? Because I expect you'll be wanting your share!"

"No," said the witch, "Not a single penny will I take. You've simply got to bring me an old tinder-box that my grandmother forgot when she was last down there."

"Oh, come on, then! Let me get that rope round my middle!" said the soldier.

"Here it is," said the witch, "and here's my blue-check apron."

Then the soldier crawled up the tree, let himself down, plump! through the hole, and now he was standing, as the witch had said, down in the great passage where the hundreds of lamps were burning.

Then he unlocked the first door. Ugh! there sat the dog with eyes as big as tea-cups and glared at him.

"You are a nice chap, you are!" said the soldier. He put it down on the witch's apron and took just as many copper pennies as he could stuff into his pockets. Then he shut the chest, put the dog up again and went into the second room. Bless my soul! there sat the dog with eyes as big as mill-wheels.

"You shouldn't stare at me so!" said the soldier; "You'll strain your eyes." And then he put the dog down on the witch's apron; but when he saw such piles of silver in the chest, he threw away all the coppers he had got and filled up his pockets and his knapsack with nothing but silver. And now he went into the third room!... Oh, but it was horrible! The dog in there had actually got two great eyes as big as the Round Tower, and they were going round and round in its head like wheels!

"Good evening!" said the soldier; and he touched his cap, because never in his life had he seen such a dog. But after he had looked at it for a bit, he thought to himself, "Enough of that!" and went and lifted the dog down on to the floor and opened the chest – why, goodness gracious, what a lot of gold there was! There was enough for him to buy the whole of Copenhagen, all the sugar-pigs that the cake-women sell, and the tin-soldiers and whips and rocking-horses in the world. Yes, yes, plenty of money in there – my word, there was!

So at once the soldier emptied out all the silver coins from his pockets and his knapsack and put in gold instead; yes, and he filled up everything with gold, his pockets, his knapsack, his cap and even his boots, so that he could hardly walk. Now he had got some money! He put the dog back on the chest, slammed the door, and then shouted up through the tree, "Hi, mother, haul me up again, will you?"

"Have you got the tinder-box?" asked the witch.

"Oh no! that's true, I had clean forgotten it," said the soldier; and he went straight back and fetched it. The witch hauled him up out of the tree, and there he was again, standing on the road with his pockets, boots, cap and knapsack bulging with money.

"What are you going to do with this tinderbox?" asked the soldier.

"That's no business of yours!" answered the witch. "You've got your money; now just give me my tinder-box!"

"Rubbish!" said the soldier. "Tell me at once what you want to do with it – or I'll have out my sword and cut your head off."

"No," said the witch.

So he cut off her head... There she lay!

But the soldier tied up all his money in her apron and made a bundle of it, to go on his back. He put the tinder-box in his pocket and went straight on into the town.

It was a fine town, and he put up at the finest inn. He ordered the very best rooms and the food he was most fond of; for, now that he had all that money, he was a rich man. The servant who had to clean his boots thought, well, this was a funny old pair of boots for such a rich gentleman to have; but he hadn't yet bought any new ones. The next day he went out and got some good boots and some really smart clothes. And now the soldier had become quite a fashionable gentleman, and they told him all about the sights of their town, and about their King, and what a pretty Princess his daughter was.

"Where is she to be seen?" asked the soldier.

"She just isn't to be seen," they all answered. "She lives in a big copper castle with lots of walls and towers all round it. No one but the King is allowed to go to her there, because a fortune-teller once said that she is to marry a common soldier, and the King doesn't like that at all."

"My word! I should like to see her," thought the soldier; but of course he couldn't possibly get leave to.

And now he lived a merry life.

He was always going to the theatre, or driving in the Park; and he gave away lots of money to the poor. That was very nice of him; you see, he remembered so well from the old days how awful it was to be absolutely penniless. But now he was rich and well-dressed, and so he made lots of friends who all said what a fine fellow he was – a real gentleman – and the soldier liked that very much. But as he was spending money every day and never getting any back, at last he had only got twopence left; and so he had to move from the fine rooms he had been living in and go and live in a little poky attic right under the roof. He had to clean his own boots and mend them with a darning-needle, and none of his friends ever came to see him, for there were such a lot of stairs to climb.

One evening, when it was quite dark and he couldn't even buy himself a candle, he suddenly remembered that there was a little bit of candle left in the tinder-box that he had got for the old witch out of the hollow tree. He got out the tinder-box and the bit of candle; but just as he was striking a light and the sparks flew up from the flint, the door sprang open, and the dog he had seen down in the tree with eyes as big as tea-cups stood before him and said "What are my lord's commands?"

"I say!" said the soldier. "This must be a queer sort of tinder-box, if I can get whatever I want like that." "Bring me some money," he said to the dog; then flick! and away it went, and flick! here it was back again, with a large bagful of pennies in its mouth.

And now the soldier realised what a splendid tinder-box it was. One stroke brought before him the dog which sat on the chest with the copper money; two strokes, the dog with the silver; and three strokes, the dog with the gold. The soldier lost no time in changing back into the fine rooms and the smart clothes, and of course all his friends remembered him again at once and were tremendously fond of him.

And then one day he thought to himself "There's something queer about this, that no one's allowed to see the Princess. She's supposed to be so very lovely, according to all these people; but what's the good of that, if she has to sit the whole time inside the copper castle, the one that has all those towers? Can't I possibly manage to see her somehow? Now then, where's my tinder-box?" So he struck a light and flick! there stood the dog with the eyes as big as tea-cups.

"Of course I know it's the middle of the night", said the soldier, "but all the same I would like to see the Princess, that I would! Just for half a jiffy!"

The dog was out of the door in a flash and, before the soldier had time to think about it, there was the dog again with the Princess lying asleep on his back; and she looked so lovely that anyone could see she was a real princess; and the soldier simply couldn't resist, he had to kiss her – he was a soldier all over.

Then the dog scuttled back again with the Princess, but in the morning, when the King and Queen were at breakfast, the Princess said she had had such a curious dream in the night, about a dog and a soldier. She had ridden on the dog's back, and the soldier had kissed her.

"That's a pretty tale, if you like!" said the Queen.

And so one of the old ladies-in-waiting was told to sit up the following night by the Princess's bed and see if it was really a dream or not.

The soldier did so long for another look at the pretty Princess; and so up came the dog by night and took her and dashed off at full speed. But the old lady-in-waiting put on her overboots and ran just as fast after them, and when she saw them disappear into a big house she thought to herself, "Now I know where it is," and chalked up a big cross on the door. Then she went home to bed, and the dog came back too with the Princess. But when it saw a cross had been chalked on the door where the soldier was living, the dog also took a bit of chalk and put a cross on every door in the town. That was a clever idea, because now, you see, the lady-in-waiting couldn't find the right door, as there were crosses on the whole lot of them.

Early in the morning the King and Queen, the old lady-in-waiting and all the Court officials sallied forth in order to see where it was the Princess had been.

"Here's the house!" said the King, when he saw the first door with a cross on it.

"No, it's there, darling!" said the Queen, catching sight of the second door with a cross on it.

"But here's another – and there's another!" they all kept saying. Whichever way they turned, there were crosses on the doors. So then they soon realised that it was no good searching any longer.

But the Queen, you know, was a very clever woman, who could do more than just drive out in a coach. She took her great golden scissors and cut up a large piece of silk and sewed the pieces together into a pretty little bag, which she filled with the finest buckwheat flour. She fastened the little bag to the Princess's back, and then she snipped a little hole in the bag, so as to sprinkle the flour wherever the Princess went. At night, up came the dog once more, took the Princess on his back and ran off with her to the soldier, who loved her so dearly and did so wish he were a prince and could marry her.

The dog never noticed how the flour kept leaking out all the way from the castle to the soldier's window, where it ran up the wall with the Princess. The next morning it was quite plain to the King and Queen where their daughter had been going; so they took the soldier and put him in prison.

There he sat. Ugh! how dark and dreary his cell was! And, beside, they kept saying to him "To-morrow you're going to be hanged!" That didn't sound at all cheerful, and the worst of it was he had left his tinder-box at the inn. In the morning, through the iron bars of his little window, he watched people hurrying out of the town to see him hanged. He heard the drums and saw the soldiers marching past. Everyone was afoot. Among them was a cobbler's boy in leather apron and slippers; he was trotting along so fast that one of his slippers came off and flew right against the wall where the soldier sat peeping out between the iron bars.

"I say! you young cobbler, you don't need to hurry like that," the soldier said to him, "They can't begin without me. But look here - if you will kindly run along to where I've been living and fetch me my tinderbox; you shall have twopence for your trouble; but mind you get a move on!" The cobbler's boy was very glad to earn twopence, so he sprinted off for the tinder-box, brought it to the soldier, and - well, now listen to what happened!

Outside the town a high gallows had been built, and round about it stood the soldiers and thousands and thousands of people. The King and Queen sat on a beautiful throne opposite the judge and all his councillors.

Already the soldier had climbed the ladder; but just as they were going to put the rope round his neck he reminded them that, before being executed, a criminal always had the right to ask for one harmless favour. He said he would so like to smoke a pipe of tobacco - after all, it would be the last pipe he could smoke in this world.

Now, the King didn't like to say no to that; so the soldier took his tinder-box and struck a light - one, two, three! - and there stood all three dogs: the one with eyes as big as tea-cups,

14

the one with eyes like mill-wheels, and the one which had eyes as big as the Round Tower.

"Save me now from being hanged!" said the soldier; and then the dogs flew at the judges and all the councillors, and seized some by their legs and others by their noses, and tossed them so high into the air that when they came down they were dashed to pieces.

"I won't be tossed!" said the King; but the biggest dog picked them both up, King and Queen, and sent them hurtling after the others. Then the soldiers got frightened, and the people all shouted out "Soldier boy, you shall be our King and have the pretty Princess." And they put the soldier into the King's coach, and all three dogs went dancing in front of it and cried out "Hurrah!" And the boys whistled on their fingers, and the soldiers presented arms. The Princess came out of the copper castle and was made Queen, and how pleased she was! The wedding-feast lasted for a week, and the dogs sat at table with everyone else and kept rolling their great big eyes.

THE DARNING NEEDLE

There was once a darning needle who was really so fine that she fancied she was a sewing needle.

"Now, do mind what you're about," said the darning needle to the fingers who picked her up. "Don't drop me! If I fall on the floor, I might never be found again, I'm so fine."

"Oh, come, come!" said the fingers. "Not as fine as that" – and squeezed her round the waist.

"Look, here I come with my retinue," said the darning needle, trailing a long thread after her; but it hadn't any knot. The fingers guided the needle straight to the cook's slipper; the leather upper was split and had now got to be repaired. "Work like this – what a come-down!" said the darning needle. "I shall never get through. I shall break, I shall break" – and break she did. "There, I told you so," said the darning needle. "I'm too fine."

Now she was no good at all, thought the fingers; but, all the same, they couldn't let go of her. The cook dropped some sealingwax on her and stuck her in the front of the scarf round her neck. "Look, now I'm a brooch," said the darning needle. "I was certain I should make my way in time. One who is something will always go far." And she laughed inside her, for you can never tell from the outside whether a darning needle is laughing. There she sat, as proudly as if she were driving in her carriage and looking all about her.

"May I venture to inquire whether you are made of gold?" she asked a pin sitting next to her. "I admire your looks – with a head of your own, too, though it's rather small. You must try and make it grow, for we can't all be waxed on one end." With that, the darning needle drew herself up so proudly that she fell off the scarf into the wash-tub, just as the cook was rinsing it out.

"Now we're off on our travels," said the darning needle. "I only hope I don't get lost." But she did.

"I'm too fine for this world," she said as she sat in the gutter. "Still, my conscience is clear, and that's always a comfort." And the darning needle held herself straight and kept up her spirits.

All sorts of things went floating over her – sticks, straws, bits of newspaper. "Look at the way they go sailing along," said the darning needle. "Little do they realize what is at the bottom of it all: I am at the bottom – here I sit!... Look, there goes a stick that thinks of nothing in the world but a 'stick', and that's what he is. There goes a straw – see how he twists and turns! Don't think so much about yourself, or you'll bump into the kerb... There goes a bit of newspaper – the news in it is all forgotten, and yet it still spreads itself... I stay patient and quiet. I know what I am, and I shan't change."

One day there was something near by shining so beautifully that the darning needle thought it was a diamond; but it proved to be a bit of broken bottle, and as it was so bright the darning needle spoke to it and introduced herself as a brooch.

"You're a diamond, aren't you?" "Well, yes – something of the sort," was the answer. And so they each thought the other to be worth a great deal, and they chatted together about how stuck-up everybody was.

"You see, I have lived in a box belonging to a young lady," said the darning needle; "and that young lady was a cook. She had five fingers on each hand, but I never knew anything like the conceit of those five fingers. They had nothing to do but to hold me – to take me out of the box and put me back again."

"Did they glitter at all?" asked the bit of broken bottle. "Glitter!" replied the darning needle. "No, they swaggered! They were five brothers, all fingers by birth. They stood up straight beside each other, though their heights were all different. First, at the end of the row, came *Tom Thumb*, who was short and fat; his place being outside the others, he had only one joint in his back and could only bow once, but he used to explain that if ever he were cut off a man's hand that man would never be taken for war service. Next came *Lick-Pot*, who found his way into sweet and sour alike, pointed at the sun and moon, and was the one who pressed on the pen when they wrote. *Longshank* looked over the others' heads. *Goldbrand* wore a gold ring round his middle, and little *Peer Playboy* did nothing at all and was proud of it. It was all swagger, nothing but swagger; and that's why I went into the wash-tub."

"And here we sit and glitter," said the bit of glass. Just then a lot more water came down the gutter, till it overflowed and carried the bit of glass away with it.

"There, now he has had a step up," said the darning needle. "I'll stay where I am – I'm too fine to move – but that's something I'm proud of; it deserves respect." So she sat there stiffly and thought her own thoughts.

"I'm so fine that, really, I might almost have been born of a sunbeam. I believe, too, that the sun regularly looks for me under the water. Oh, I'm so fine that my own mother can't discover me; if I had my old eye, which broke, I really believe I should cry – though of course I couldn't do that; one doesn't cry."

One day some street boys were fishing about in the gutter, where they came across old nails, ha'pennies and things of that sort. It was a messy occupation, but it was just what they enjoyed.

"Ow!" cried one of them – he had pricked himself on the darning needle. "I say, what a beast of a thing!"

"I'm not a beast, or a thing; I'm a young lady," said the darning needle. But nobody heard her; the sealing-wax had come off, and she had turned black. But black is so slimming, and so she fancied herself finer than ever.

"Here comes an eggshell on the water," cried the boys; and then they stuck the darning needle into the shell.

"A white background – and me in black!" said the darning needle. "How becoming! Well, now they can see me... I do hope I shan't be seasick, for then I should break." Well, she wasn't seasick, and she didn't break.

"A steel stomach is just the thing to prevent seasickness and also a reminder that one's a bit above the common herd. I've

quite recovered. The finer you are, the more you can put up with."

"Crunch!" went the eggshell, as a cart ran over it. "Ooh! what a squeeze!" said the darning needle. "Now I *am* seasick – I'm breaking!" But she didn't break, in spite of being run over by the cart. She was lying at full length – and there she may as well stay.

THE STAUNCH
TIN SOLDIER

There were once twenty-five tin soldiers, all brothers, for they all came from one old tin spoon. "Shoulder arms! Eyes front!" – that's how they were, and they wore splendid red tunics with blue trousers. The very first thing they ever heard, when the lid was taken off the box in which they were lying, was – "tin soldiers!" It was a little boy who shouted this and clapped his hands. He had been given them for his birthday, and now he was putting them up on the table.

Each soldier was the very image of the other, except for one who was a little bit different. He had only one leg, because he was the last to be made and there wasn't enough tin to go round. Still, there he stood, as firmly on his one leg as the others on their two; and, as it happened, he's the soldier this story is all about.

There were a lot of other toys on the table where the tin soldiers had been put up, but the one you noticed first was a beautiful paper castle; through its tiny windows you could see right into the rooms. In front of it were some small trees standing round a little mirror, which was supposed to represent a lake, with wax swans reflected in it as they swam. Everything was very pretty, and yet the prettiest of all was a little lady who was standing at the open door of the castle. She, too, was cut out of paper, but she was wearing a skirt of the clearest muslin and a narrow blue ribbon draped over her shoulder like a scarf, with a glittering spangle in the middle as big as the whole of her face. The little lady was holding out both her arms; you see, she was a dancer and, besides, she had kicked one of her legs so high in the air that the tin soldier couldn't make out where it was and imagined she only had one leg, like himself.

"That's the wife for me!" he thought to himself. "But she's so grand; she lives in a castle. I've only got a box, and there are twenty-five of us to that; it's no place for her. All the same, I must see if I can't get to know her." Then he lay down at full length behind a snuff-box that was on the table. From here he could keep his eyes on the elegant little lady, who continued to stand on one leg without losing her balance.

Later in the evening, all the other tin soldiers went back into their box, and the people in the house went to bed. The toys now began to play games – visiting, fighting, dancing. The tin soldiers rattled in their box, because they wanted to join in, but they couldn't get the lid off. The nutcrackers turned somersaults, and the slate pencil had some fun on the slate. There was such a noise that the canary woke up and began to join in with some twittering in verse. The only two who didn't budge were the tin soldier and the little dancer. She stood perfectly upright on tiptoe with both arms stretched out, while he was just as staunch on his one leg; his eyes never left her for a moment.

Suddenly the clock struck twelve and – clack! flew the lid from the snuff-box, but do you suppose there was snuff in it? No, there was a little black goblin – it was a kind of Jack-in-the-box.

"Tin soldier!" cried the goblin. "Will you please keep your eyes to yourself!" But the tin soldier pretended not to hear.

"All right – you wait till tomorrow!" said the goblin.

And when tomorrow came and the children got up, the tin soldier was put away by the window; and, whether it was the goblin or the draught that did it, all at once the window flew open and the soldier fell out head first from the third storey. It was a terrible fall. There was his leg going straight up in the air, and he was left standing on his helmet with his bayonet stuck in between the paving-stones.

The maidservant and the little boy came down directly to look for him; but although they very nearly trod on him, they never saw him. If only the tin soldier had called out "Here I am!" they would have found him easily enough; but he didn't think it would be right to shout out, as he was in uniform.

Presently it began raining, more and more heavily, until it was a regular downpour. When it was over, two street-boys came by. "Gosh, look at that!" said one of them. "There's a tin soldier. Let's send him for a sail." So they made a boat out of a newspaper, put the tin soldier aboard, and away he sailed down the gutter with the two boys running alongside and clapping their hands. Bless my soul, how the waves did rock in the gutter, and what a strong current there was! Well, after all, it had been a real soaker. The paper boat bobbed up and down, and now and then it whirled round so fast that the tin soldier became quite dizzy. But he kept staunch and never moved a muscle; he looked straight ahead, and still shouldered arms.

All at once the boat drifted in under a broad culvert; it was as dark as if he were in his box.

"I wonder where I'm coming to now", he thought. "I'll swear it's all the fault of that goblin. If only the little lady were here in the boat, it could be twice as dark for all I'd care!"

Just then a great water-rat appeared, who lived under the culvert. "Where's your passport?" asked the rat. "Now then, show me your passport!"

But the tin soldier never said a word and clutched his gun more tightly than ever. The boat rushed on, and the rat after it. Ugh! How it ground its teeth and shouted out to sticks and straws: "Stop him! Stop him! He hasn't paid the toll! He hasn't shown his passport!"

But the current grew stronger and stronger; the tin soldier could already see daylight ahead where the culvert ended. But he could also hear a roaring sound that might well bring dismay to the bravest man. Just think of it – where the culvert ended, the gutter plunged straight out into a large canal. It was as dangerous for him as it would be for us to sail down a big waterfall.

By now he had come so near that there was no stopping. The boat dashed out, the poor tin soldier held himself as stiffly as he could; no one should say that he had moved an eyelid. The boat spun round three or four times and filled right up, with water, until it was bound to sink. The tin soldier was now up to his neck; the boat sank deeper and deeper; the paper grew more and more sodden. At last the water closed over the soldier's head... He thought of the pretty little dancer whom he would never see again, and the old song rang in his ears:

"On, on, brave warrior!

On, where death awaits thee!"

At this moment, the paper went to pieces, and the tin soldier fell right through – but was instantly swallowed by a large fish. Oh, and how dark it was inside! Even worse than it was in the culvert, and so terribly cramped, too. But the tin soldier was still staunch, still shouldering arms, as he lay at full length.

The fish darted about, making the most terrifying twists and turns. Then at last it lay quite still; a lightning flash went through it, there was broad daylight, and someone called out: "A tin soldier!" The fish had been caught, taken to market and sold, and here it was in the kitchen, where the maid cut it open with a big knife. She picked up the soldier by the waist with her two fingers and carried him into the parlour, where everyone wanted to see this extraordinary man who had been travelling about inside a fish. But the tin soldier thought nothing of it. They set him up on the table, and there – well, what wonderful things can happen! The tin soldier found himself in the very same room as he had been in before. There they were – the same children, the same toys on the table, the same beautiful castle with the pretty little dancer who still stood on one leg and kept the other one high in the air – she, too, had been staunch. This touched the tin soldier, who could have wept tears of tin, only that would hardly have done! He looked at her, and she looked at him, but neither of them spoke.

Suddenly one of the small boys took and threw the soldier straight into the stove. He had no reason for doing this; of course, the Jack-in-the-box was behind it all.

The tin soldier stood in a complete glow; the heat that he felt was tremendous, but whether it came from the actual fire or from love, he had no idea. All his bright colours were gone, but no one could tell if this had happened on his voyage or was the result of grief. He looked at the little lady, she looked at him, and he could feel that he was melting, but he still stood staunchly with arms at the shoulder. Then a door opened, the draught caught the dancer, and she flew like a sylph right into the stove to the tin soldier, flared up in a flame and was gone. The tin soldier was melted down to a lump and, when the maid cleared out the ashes next morning, she found him in the shape of a little tin heart; but all that was left of the dancer was her spangle, and that was burnt as black as coal.

THE SHEPHERDESS AND
THE CHIMNEY-SWEEP

Have you ever seen a real old-fashioned cupboard, its wood quite black with age and carved all over with twirls and twisting foliage? There was one just like that in a certain sitting-room. It had been left by a great-grandmother and was carved from top to bottom with roses and tulips and the quaintest flourishes, and in among were little stags poking out their heads that were covered with antlers. But, carved on the middle of the cupboard, was the complete figure of a man; he really did look comic. And his grin was comic, too – you couldn't call it a laugh – and he had billygoat legs, little horns on his forehead and a long beard. The children who lived there always called him "Major-and-Minor-General-Company-Sergeant Billygoatlegs", because it was a difficult name to say, and there aren't many who get that rank. What a job it must have been to carve him out! Well, anyhow, there he was; and all the time he kept looking at the table under the

27

looking-glass, for there stood a lovely little china shepherdess. She had gilt shoes, a frock that was charmingly caught up with a red rose, and a gold hat and shepherd's crook; she was delicious. Close beside her was a little chimney-sweep, as black as coal, though he too was made of china. He was just as trim and tidy as anyone else, for he really only pretended to be a chimney-sweep; the man who made him could just as well have made him a prince, for that matter.

There he stood, looking so smart with his ladder and with cheeks as pink and white as a girl's. That was really a mistake; better if he'd been just a little bit sooty. He was standing quite close to the shepherdess; they had both been placed where they were and, because of that, they had become engaged. They certainly suited each other: they were both young, both made of the same china, and both equally brittle.

Near them, three times their size, was another figure – an old Chinaman who could nod. He too was made of porcelain, and he said he was the little shepherdess's grandfather, though he couldn't prove it. Still, he claimed to be her guardian; and so, when Major-and-Minor-General-Company-Sergeant Billygoatlegs had asked for the hand of the little shepherdess, the old Chinaman nodded his consent.

"There's a husband for you," he said; "a husband I'm almost sure is made of mahogany. He will make you Mrs. Major-and-Minor-General-Company-Sergeant Billygoatlegs. That cupboard of his is full of silver, to say nothing of what he has stowed away secretly."

"I won't go into that dark cupboard," said the little shepherdess. "I've heard that he's got eleven porcelain wives in there already."

"Then you can be the twelfth," said the Chinaman. "Tonight, as soon as ever the old cupboard starts creaking, you two shall be married – as sure as I'm a Chinese." And then with another nod he went off to sleep.

But the little shepherdess was in tears and looked at her darling sweetheart, the porcelain chimney-sweep. "I've something to ask you," she said. "Will you come with me out into the wide world? We can't possibly stay here."

"I'll do whatever you like," said the chimney-sweep. "Let's go at once; I feel sure I can earn enough at my job to support you."

"How I wish we were safely down from this table!" she said. "I shan't be happy till we're out in the wide world."

He did his best to console her, and he showed her how to put her little foot on the carved ledges and the gilded tracery that went winding round the leg of the table; and he also used his ladder to help her, and there they were at last on the floor. But when they looked across at the old cupboard, there was such a to-do. All the carved stags were poking out their heads and pricking up their antlers and twisting their necks. Major-and-Minor-General-Company-Sergeant Billygoatlegs jumped right up and shouted across to the old Chinaman, "Look! They're running away, they're running away!"

That gave them a bit of a scare, and they quickly popped into the drawer under the window-seat. They found three or four packs of cards in there, one of them complete, and a little toy-theatre that had been put together after a fashion. They were doing a play, and all the Queens – hearts and diamonds, clubs and spades – sat in the front row fanning themselves with their tulips, while behind them stood all the Knaves showing that they had heads both top and bottom, as they do on cards. The play was about a couple who weren't allowed to get married, and it made the shepherdess cry, because that was her story all over again.

"I can't bear it," she said. "I must get out of this drawer." But when they reached the floor and looked up at the table, the old

29

Chinaman had woken up; his whole body was swaying to and fro, for, you see, the lower part of him was all one piece.

"Here comes the old Chinaman!" shrieked the little shepherdess, and she was in such a way that she sank down on her porcelain knees.

"I've got an idea," said the chimney-sweep. "Let's crawl down into the big pot-pourri jar over there in the corner; we can lie there on roses and lavender and throw salt in his eyes when he comes."

"That wouldn't be any good," she said. "Besides, I know the old Chinaman and the pot-pourri jar used to be engaged; and there's always a little tenderness left over, once people have been like that to each other. No, there's nothing for it but to go out into the wide world."

"Are you really as brave as that – to come out with me into the wide world?" asked the chimney-sweep. "Do you realise how huge it is, and that we can never come back here again?"

"I do," she answered.

Then the chimney-sweep looked her full in the face and said, "My way lies through the chimney. Are you really as brave as that – to crawl with me through the stove, past firebricks and flue, till we come out into the chimney? Once we're there, I know what I'm doing. We shall climb so high that they can't get at us, and right at the very top there's a hole leading out into the wide world."

And he led her up to the door of the stove.

"It does look black," she said; but she went with him all the same, past firebricks and flue, and where it was pitch-dark.

"Now we're in the chimney," he said, "and, look, there is the loveliest star shining overhead!"

Yes, it was a real star in the sky, shining straight down to them, just as though it wanted to show them the way. And they crawled and crept – it was a horrible climb – up and up. But he kept lifting and helping and holding her, pointing out the best places for her to put her little china feet. And at last they got right up to the top of the chimney and sat down on the edge, for they were tired out, and no wonder.

There was the sky with all its stars over-head, and the town with all its roofs below them. They could see round in every direction, far out into the world. The poor shepherdess had never imagined it was like that; she laid her little head on the chimney-sweep's shoulder and cried and cried till the gold ran from her sash.

"This is too much!" she said. "I can't bear it – the world's far too big. If only I were back on the little table under the looking-glass! I shall never be happy until I'm there again. I've come with you into the wide world; now I want you to take me home again, if you love me at all."

The chimney-sweep tried every argument. He reminded her of the old Chinaman and of Major-and-Minor-General-Company-Sergeant Billygoatlegs; but she sobbed so bitterly and kept kissing her little chimney-sweep, so that at last he had to give way to her, wrong as it was.

Then with great difficulty they crawled down the chimney again, crept through the flue and the firebricks – it wasn't at all nice – and there they stood in the dark stove, lurking behind the door so as to find out what was going on in the room. There wasn't a sound. They peeped out... goodnesss gracious! There in the middle of the floor lay the old Chinaman. In trying to run after them he had fallen off the table and was lying there smashed into three fragments. The whole of his back had come off in a single piece, and his head had bowled away into a corner. Major-and-Minor-General-Company-Sergeant Billygoatlegs stood where he had always stood, in deep thought.

"How dreadful!" cried the little shepherdess. "Old Grandpa's broken, and it's all our fault. I shall never get over it." And she wrung her tiny hands.

"He can still be riveted," said the chimney-sweep. "He can quite well be riveted. Now, don't get so worked up. When they've glued his back for him and given him a nice rivet in the neck, he'll be as good as new again and able to say all sorts of nasty things to us."

"Do you think so?" she said – and then they clambered up on to the table where they had been standing before.

"Well, here we are back where we started," said the chimneysweep. "We might have saved ourselves all that trouble."

"I do wish we had old Grandpa safely riveted," said the shepherdess. "Do you think it'll be very expensive?"

He was mended all right. The family had his back glued, and he was given a nice rivet in the neck. He was as good as new – but he couldn't nod.

"You *have* become high and mighty since you got broken," said Major-and-Minor-General-Company-Sergeant Billygoat-legs. "Yet I can't see that it's anything to be so proud of. Well – am I to have her, or am I not?"

It was touching to see how the chimney-sweep and the little shepherdess looked at the old Chinaman; they were so afraid he might nod. But he couldn't do that, and he didn't like to have to explain to a stranger that he had a rivet in his neck for good and all. So the porcelain couple stayed together; and they blessed Grandfather's rivet and went on loving each other until at last they got broken.

THE SWINEHERD

Once upon a time there was a prince who hadn't much money, but he had a kingdom; and though this was quite small, it was large enough to marry on, and marry he would.

Still, it was really rather bold of him to say straight out to the Emperor's daughter: "Will you have me?" But sure enough he did, for his name was famous everywhere, and there were hundreds of princesses who would only too gladly have taken him. But do you think she did? Well, now just listen. Growing on the grave of the Prince's father was a rose-tree – oh, such a lovely rose-tree. It only flowered every five years, and even then had but one solitary bloom. But this rose smelt so sweet that it made you forget all your cares and troubles. And the Prince also had a nightingale that could sing just as if it had all the loveliest tunes hidden away in its little throat. The Princess should have both the rose and the nightingale, he said; and so they were placed in big silver caskets and sent to her.

The Emperor had them brought before him in the great hall, where the Princess was playing "visitors" with her maids-of-honour. They never did anything else and, when she saw the big caskets with the presents inside, she clapped her hands with glee.

"I do hope it's a pussy-cat," she said... But then out came the lovely rose.

"Oh, isn't it pretty!" cried all the maids-of-honour.

"It's more than pretty," said the Emperor, "It's handsome."

But when the Princess touched it she nearly burst into tears. "Oh, Papa, what a shame!" she cried. "It's not artificial, it's real!"

"Come, let's first see what's in the other casket before we get annoyed," suggested the Emperor. And then out came the nightingale. Its singing was so lovely that for the moment there wasn't a thing that could be said against it.

"*Superbe! Charmant!*" exclaimed the maids-of-honour, for they all talked French, the one worse than the other. "How the bird reminds me of Her late Majesty's musicalbox!" said an old courtier. "Dear me, yes! Exactly the same tone, the same expression!"

"So it is," said the Emperor; and he cried like a child.

"All the same, I can't believe that it's real," said the Princess.

"Yes, it is; it's a real live bird," said the ones who had brought it.

"All right, then let it fly away," said the Princess, and she wouldn't hear of the Prince being allowed to come.

But he wasn't going to be put off like that. He smeared his face with brown and black, pulled his cap down over his eyes and knocked at the door. "Good morning, Emperor!" he said. "I wonder if you've got a job for me here at the Castle."

"Ah, well," said the Emperor, "there are so many who come and ask that. But now, let me see – yes, I want some one to mind the pigs. We've such a lot of pigs."

And so the Prince was appointed Imperial Swineherd. He was given a miserable little room down by the pig-sties, and there he had to live. But all day he sat working, and by the evening he had made a lovely little pot with bells round it and, as soon as the pot boiled, these tinkled charmingly; they played the old tune of -

>"Ah, my dear Augustine,
>Our dreams are all done, done, done!"

But the cunningest arrangement of all was that, if you held your finger in the steam from the pot, you could at once smell what was being cooked on every fire in the town. Well, of course, that was something quite different from a rose.

Presently the Princess came strolling along with all her courtladies, and when she heard the music she stopped, looking so delighted; for she, too, could play "Ah, my dear Augustine" – it was the only tune she knew, and she played it with one finger.

"Why, that's *my* tune!" she said. "This pigman must be a man of taste. Look here, go in and ask him how much he wants for the instrument."

So one of the court-ladies had to run in and see him; but she put on her clogs first.

"How much do you want for that pot?" she asked.

"I want ten kisses from the Princess," answered the pigman.

"Goodness gracious!" said the maid-of-honour.

"That's the price; I can't take less," said the pigman.

"Well, what does he say?" asked the Princess.

"I really can't repeat it," said the maid-of-honour. "It's too dreadful."

"Well, then whisper it" – and the maid-of-honour whispered it.

"Oh, how rude he is!" said the Princess and walked off at once. But when she had gone a little way, the bells began to tinkle so charmingly -

"Ah, my dear Augustine,
Our dreams are all done, done, done!"

"Come," said the Princess, "ask him if he will take ten kisses from my ladies-in-waiting."

"No, thank you," said the pigman. "Ten kisses from the Princess, or I stick to my pot!"

"How horribly annoying!" said the Princess. "Well, then, you ladies'll have to stand in front of me, so that no one can see."

The court-ladies went and stood in front of her, spreading out their dresses; and then the pigman had his ten kisses and she got her pot.

Goodness! What fun they had! Day and night the pot was kept on the boil. There wasn't a kitchen in the town where they didn't know what was being cooked, whether it was the Mayor's or the shoemaker's. The maids-of-honour danced about, clapping their hands with glee.

"We know who's going to have soup and pancakes, and we know who's going to have chops and jelly. It's so interesting."

"Most interesting," observed the high Stewardess.

"Yes, but not a word to anyone, mind you; for I'm the Emperor's daughter."

"O, dear, no!" they all replied. "We shouldn't dream of it."

The swineherd - that is to say, the Prince, but you see, they didn't know but that he was a regular pigman - couldn't let the day go by without making something. The next thing he made was a rattle. When you swung it round, it played all the waltzes and jigs and polkas that anybody had ever heard of.

"Now that really is *superbe*," said the Princess, as she was passing. "I've never heard anything lovelier. Look here, go in and ask him what he wants for that instrument. But, mind, no kisses!"

"He wants a hundred kisses from the Princess," said the lady-in-waiting who had been in to ask.

"The fellow must be mad," said the Princess and began to walk off. But when she had gone a little way, she stopped. "Art must be encouraged," she said; "after all, I'm the Emperor's daughter. Tell him he shall have ten kisses like yesterday, and my ladies-in-waiting will give him the rest."

"Oh, but we couldn't bear to do that," said the ladies.

"Nonsense!" said the Princess. "If I can kiss him, so can you. Remember, I give you wages and board" – and once more the maid-of-honour had to go in and see the pigman.

"A hundred kisses from the Princess," he said, "or we stay as we are."

"Stand in front!" she cried. And so all the court-ladies placed themselves in front, and the kissing began.

"What on earth are they all up to over there by the sties!" said the Emperor, who had just stepped out on to his balcony. He rubbed his eyes and put on his spectacles. "Why, it's the ladies-in-waiting, up to some game or other. Perhaps I'd better go and have a look" – and he gave a hitch to the back of his slippers, for he had trodden them down at the heel.

Phew! What a hurry he was in!

As soon as he came down into the courtyard, he crept along very quietly. And the maids-of-honour were so busy counting the kisses, for it had to be fair do's – he mustn't have too many kisses, nor yet too few – that they never noticed the Emperor, who now drew himself up on tiptoe.

"What's all this!" he said, when he saw them kissing; and he slogged them over the head with his slipper, just as the young pigman was having his eighty-sixth kiss. "Out you get!" said the

Emperor, for he was furious, and both Princess and swineherd were turned out of his kingdom.

Look, there she sat crying, while the swineherd scolded and the rain came down in torrents.

"Poor me!" said the Princess. "If only I had accepted the handsome Prince! Oh, I am so unhappy!"

The swineherd went behind a tree, wiped off the black and brown from his face, threw away his old clothes and now stepped forward in princely robes that were so magnificent that the Princess couldn't help making a curtsey.

"My dear, I've come to despise you," he said. "An honest prince you rejected. The rose and the nightingale were not to your taste. But the swineherd – you could kiss him for the sake of a musical box. Now you can have what you asked for!"

And with that he went into his kingdom, shut the door and bolted it; but she could stand outside if she cared to and sing -

"Ah, my dear Augustine,
Our dreams are all done, done, done!"

IT'S ABSOLUTELY TRUE!

"It's a terrible affair!" said a hen – speaking, too, in quite another part of the town from where it all happened. It's a terrible affair about that chicken-house. I daren't sleep alone tonight. It's a good thing there are so many of us roosting together." And then she told them her story, which made the other hens' feathers stand on end and even set the cock's comb drooping. It's absolutely true!

But let's begin at the beginning. It was in a chicken-house at the other end of the town. The sun went down, and the hens flew up. One of them was a white short-legged bird, who regularly laid her eggs and was altogether a most respectable hen. When she got to her perch she preened herself with her beak, and a little feather came out and went fluttering down. "So much for that one!" she said. "The more I preen, the lovelier I shall grow, no doubt!" Of course it was only said in fun, because she was the fun-maker among the hens, though in other ways (as you've just heard) most respectable. After that, she went off to sleep.

All about was quite dark; hen sat with hen, but the one next to her was still awake. She had heard, and had not heard – as you must often do in this world, if you are to live in peace and quiet. And yet she couldn't help saying to the hen perched on the other side of her, "Did you hear that? I give no names, but there is a hen who means to pluck out her feathers for the sake of her looks. If I were a cock, I'd simply despise her."

Now directly above the hens sat the owl, with her owl husband and her owl children. They had sharp ears in that family; they could hear every word their hen neighbour said; and they rolled their eyes, and the owl mother fanned herself with her wings. "Don't take any notice – but of course you heard what she said, didn't you? I heard it with my own ears, and they're going to hear a lot before they drop off. One of the hens has so far forgotten what is fit and proper for a hen that she's calmly plucking out all her feathers in full view of the cock."

"*Prenez garde aux enfants!*" said the father owl. "Not in the children's hearing!"

"But I must tell the owl over the way; she's so highly respected in our set." And away flew the mother.

"Tu-whit, tu-who!" they both hooted, and it carried right down to the doves in the dovecot across the yard. "Have you heard, have you heard? To-who! There's a hen that's plucked out all her feathers for the sake of the cock. She'll freeze to death, if she isn't dead already, tu-who!"

"Where, ooh, where?" cooed the doves.

"In the yard opposite. I as good as saw it with my own eyes. Really the story's almost too improper to repeat; but it's absolutely true."

"Tr-rue, tr-rue, every wor-rd!" said the doves; and they cooed down to their hen-run, "There's a hen, some say there are *two*, who have plucked out all their feathers so as to look different from the others and to attract the attention of the cock. It's a risky thing to do; suppose they catch cold and die of fever... Yes, they're dead – *two* of them."

Then the cock joined in: "Wake up, wake up!" he crowed, and flew up on to the wooden fence. His eyes were still sleepy, but he crowed away all the same; "Three hens have died of love for a cock; they had plucked out all their feathers. It's a horrible story – I don't want it – pass it on!" "Pass it on!" squeaked the bats; and the hens clucked and the cocks crowed, "Pass it on, pass it on!" And so the story flew from one hen-house to another, till at last it came back to the place where it had really started.

"There are five hens" – that's how it ran – "who have all plucked out their feathers to show which of them had got thinnest for love of the cock. Then they pecked at each other till the blood came and they all fell down dead, to the shame and disgrace of their family and the serious loss of their owner."

The hen that had lost the one loose little feather didn't of course recognize her own story and, as she was a respectable hen, she said, "How I despise those hens! – though there are plenty more just like them. That's not the kind of thing to be hushed up, and I shall do my best to get the story into the papers, so that it may go all over the country. It'll serve those hens right, and their family too."

And into the papers it came – all there in print – and it's absolutely true: "*One little feather can easily become five hens!*"

THUMBELINA

There was once a woman who did so want to have a wee child of her own, but she had no idea where she was to get it from. So she went off to an old witch and said to her, "I would so dearly like to have a little child. Do please tell me where I can find one."

"Oh, that!" said the witch, "Nothing easier. Take this barley-corn – mind you, it's not the kind that grows out in the fields or that the fowls are fed with. Put it in a flower-pot, and see what happens!"

"Thank you very much", said the woman, giving the witch a shilling. She went straight home and planted the barleycorn, and in no time there came up a lovely great flower which looked just like a tulip, only the petals were shut tight as though it were still in bud.

"It *is* a pretty flower," said the woman, and she gave the lovely red and yellow petals a kiss; but directly she kissed it, the flower burst open with a pop. It was a real tulip – that was plain enough now – but, sitting on the green pistil in the middle of

43

the flower, was a tiny little girl. She was delicately pretty and no taller than your thumb, so she was given the name of Thumbelina.

A nicely varnished walnut-shell did for her cradle, blue violet petals for her mattress, and a rose-leaf for her counterpane. That was where she slept at night; but in the daytime she played about on the table, where the woman had put a plate with a wreath of flowers. These dipped their stalks down into the water, in the middle of which floated a large tulip petal where Thumbelina could sit and row herself from one side of the plate to the other, using a couple of white horsehairs as oars. It was a most charming sight. She could sing, too, in the sweetest little voice you ever heard.

One night, as she lay in her pretty bed, a hideous toad came hopping in through a broken pane in the window. It was a great ugly slimy toad, and it jumped straight down on to the table where Thumbelina was lying asleep under her red rose-leaf.

"She would make a nice wife for my son," thought the toad, and she snatched up the walnut-shell in which Thumbelina was sleeping and hopped off with her through the window into the garden.

There was a wide brook running through it, but the bank was swampy and muddy, and here the toad lived with her son. Ugh! wasn't he ugly and horrible – just like his mother! "Koax, koax, brekke-ke-kex" was all he could say, when he saw the pretty little girl in the walnut-shell.

"Sh! Not so loud, or you'll wake her," said the old toad. "She might yet run away from us, for she's as light as swan's-down. Let's put her out in the brook on one of those broad water-lilies. She's so small and light that its leaf will be like an island for her. She can't escape from there, and in the meantime we'll get the best room ready under the mud for you two to live in."

There were quite a lot of water-lilies growing on the water

with their broad green leaves which seem to be floating on the surface. The biggest of them all happened to be the furthest away, but the old toad swam out and placed the walnut-shell on it with Thumbelina still sleeping inside.

Early the next morning the poor little thing woke up and, when she saw where she was, she began to cry bitterly, for the big green leaf had water all round it and she couldn't possibly reach the bank.

The old toad stayed down in the mud and decorated her room with rushes and yellow water-lilies, so as to make everything quite snug for her new daughter-in-law. Then she swam out with her son to the waterlily where Thumbelina was standing, for they wanted to fetch that fine walnut bed and put it up in the bridal-chamber before she came herself. The old toad made a low curtsey to her in the water and said, "Here's my son – he's to be your husband. You'll have a lovely home together down in the mud."

"Koax, koax, brekke-ke-kex!" was all that the son could say.

Then they took the pretty little bed and swam away with it. But Thumbelina sat all alone on the green leaf and cried, for she didn't want to live with the horrible toad or to marry her ugly son. The little fishes, swimming down there in the water, had caught sight of the toad and heard what she said. So they poked their heads out of the water; they were so anxious to have a look at the little girl. Directly they saw her, they found her charming, and they couldn't bear to think that she must go and live with the ugly toad. No, that must never happen! They all swarmed together down in the water round the green stalk that held the leaf she was standing on and gnawed it through with their teeth; whereupon the leaf floated away with Thumbelina down the brook, far away where the toad could never reach her.

Thumbelina went sailing past all sorts of places, and the little birds perched in the bushes saw her and trilled out, "What a

45

pretty little lady!" The leaf that carried her floated further and further on; and thus it was that Thumbelina began her journey abroad.

A dainty little white butterfly kept on fluttering round and round her, till at last it settled on the leaf, for it had taken a great liking to Thumbelina; and she too was pleased, because the toad couldn't reach her now and she was sailing through such a lovely part of the brook. The sunshine gleamed on the water like the finest gold. Then she took her sash and tied one end of it round the butterfly, while the other end she made fast to the leaf; and this at once gathered speed – and so did Thumbelina because, you see, she was standing on the leaf. Just then a large cockchafer came flying up and, catching sight of her, clutched her round her slender waist and flew with her up into a tree. But the green leaf went floating on and the butterfly with it, because it had been tied to the leaf and couldn't manage to free itself.

Gracious, what a fright it gave poor Thumbelina, when the cockchafer flew up into the tree with her! Still, what upset her even more was the thought of the pretty white butterfly that she had tied to the leaf; for unless it could manage to free itself, it would certainly starve to death. But that didn't worry the cockchafer in the slightest. He settled beside her on the largest green leaf in the tree, gave her some nectar from the blossoms and said how pretty she was, although she wasn't a bit like a cockchafer. Later on, all the other cockchafers living in the tree came to call on her. They stared at Thumbelina, and the young lady cockchafers shrugged their feelers – "Why, she's only got two legs," they said. "What a pitiable sight!" "She hasn't any feelers," they went on. "She's so pinched in at the waist – ugh! she might almost be a human. Isn't she ugly!" exclaimed all the lady cockchafers. And yet Thumbelina was really so pretty. And that's what the cockchafer thought who had carried her off; but

when all the others kept saying how ugly she was, then at length
he thought so too and would have nothing to do with her; she
could go where she liked. They flew with her down from the tree
and sat her on a daisy. There she cried and cried, because she
was so ugly that the cockchafers wouldn't have her; and all the
time she was as beautiful as can be – as exquisite as the loveliest
rose-petal.

Right through the summer poor Thumbelina lived quite
alone in that enormous wood. She took blades of grass and
plaited herself a bed, which she hung under a large dock-leaf, so
as to be out of the rain. She got her food from the honey in the
flowers, and her drink from the morning dew on the leaves; and
in this way summer and autumn went by. But now came winter
– the long, cold winter. All the birds that had sung to her so
beautifully now flew away; the trees and flowers withered; the
great dockleaf she had been living under furled itself into nothing but a faded yellow stalk. She felt the cold most terribly, for
her clothes were by this time in tatters, and she herself was so
tiny and delicate, poor Thumbelina, that she would surely be
frozen to death. It began snowing, and every snowflake that fell
on her was like a whole shovelful being thrown on us, for we are
quite big and she was no taller than your thumb. So she
wrapped herself up in a dead leaf, but there was no warmth in
that, and she shivered with cold.

On the fringe of the wood where she had now come to was a
large cornfield; but the corn had long been harvested, and only
the bare barren stubble thrust up from the frozen earth. It was
just like an entire forest for her to walk through – oh, and she
was shivering with cold! At length she came to the field-
mouse's door. It was a little hole down below the stubble. There
the field-mouse had a fine snug place to live in, with a whole
roomful of corn and a splendid kitchen and dining-room. Poor
Thumbelina stood just inside the door like any other wretched

beggar-girl and asked for a little bit of barleycorn, for she hadn't had a scrap to eat for two days.

"You poor mite!" said the field-mouse, for at heart she was a kind old thing. "Come you in and have a bite with me in my warm room."

As she at once took a liking to Thumbelina she made a suggestion. "You're quite welcome to stay with me for the winter," she said, "as long as you'll keep my rooms nice and tidy and also tell me stories, for I'm so fond of stories." And Thumbelina did what the kind old field-mouse asked for and was extremely comfortable there.

"I dare say we shall have a visitor before long," said the field-mouse. "My neighbour generally pays me a call once a week. His house is even snugger than mine, with goodsized rooms, and he wears such a lovely black velvet coat. If only you could get him for a husband, you'd be comfortably off. But his sight's very bad. You must tell him all the nicest stories you know."

Thumbelina took no notice of all this; she had no intention of marrying the neighbour, for he was a mole. He came and called in his black velvet coat. He was so rich and clever, according to the field-mouse, and his home was twenty times the size of the fieldmouse's. He was very learned, but he couldn't bear sunshine and pretty flowers; he said all sorts of nasty things about them, never having seen them. Thumbelina had to sing, and she sang both "Ladybird, ladybird, fly away home" and "Ring-a-ring-o'roses"; and the mole fell in love with her because of her pretty voice, but he didn't say anything – he was much too cautious a man for that.

He had lately dug a long passage for himself through the earth, leading from his house to theirs. Here the field-mouse and Thumbelina were invited to stroll whenever they cared to. But he told them not to be afraid of the dead bird lying in the passage; it was a whole bird with beak and feathers, that had evidently only just died as the winter began and was now buried in the very spot where he had made his underground passage.

The mole took a bit of touchwood in his mouth – for in the dark that shines just like fire – and went ahead to give them a light in the long dark passage. When they came to where the dead bird was lying, the mole tilted his broad snout up to the ceiling and thrust through the earth; making a large hole through which the light could penetrate. In the middle of the floor lay a dead swallow with its pretty wings folded close in to its sides, and head and legs tucked in beneath its feathers. The poor bird must have died of cold. Thumbelina felt so sorry for it; she was very fond of all the little birds that had sung and twittered for her so sweetly right through the summer. But the mole kicked at it with his stumpy legs, saying, "That won't chirp any more! How wretched it must be to be born a little bird! Thank goodness no child of mine ever will be. A bird like that has of course nothing but its twitter and is bound to starve to death when winter comes."

"Just what I'd expect to hear from a sensible man like you," said the field-mouse. "What has a bird to show for all its twittering, when winter comes? It must starve and freeze. But I suppose that's considered a great thing."

Thumbelina didn't say a word, but when the other two turned their back on the bird, she stooped down and, smoothing aside the feathers that lay over its head, she kissed its closed eyes. "Who knows – this may be the very one," she thought, "that used to sing so beautifully to me last summer."

The mole now filled in the hole where the daylight shone through and saw the two ladies home. But that night Thumbelina simply couldn't sleep; so she got up, and plaited a fine big blanket of hay, which she carried down and spread all over the dead bird, and she took some soft cotton-wool she had found in the field-mouse's room and tucked this in at the sides, so that the bird might lie warm in the cold earth.

"Goodbye, you lovely little bird," she said. "Goodbye, and thank you for your beautiful singing last summer, when all the trees were green and the sun was so bright and warm." Then she laid her head up against the bird's breast – but at the same moment she got such a fright, for she heard a kind of thumping inside. It was the bird's heart. The bird wasn't dead; it had been lying numb and unconscious and now, as it grew warm again, it revived.

You see, in autumn the swallows all fly away to the warm countries, but if there's one that lags behind it gets so cold that it falls down dead. There it lies, where it fell, and the cold snow covers it over.

Thumbelina was all of a tremble from the fright she had, for the bird was of course an immense great creature beside her, who was no taller than your thumb. However, she took courage and tucked the cottonwool still more closely round the poor swallow and fetched a curled mint leaf that she had been using herself for a counterpane and spread this over the bird's head.

The following night she again stole down to the bird, and this time it had quite revived; but it was so feeble that it could only open its eyes for a short moment to look at Thumbelina, standing there with a bit of touchwood in her hand, for she had no other light.

"Thank you, my darling child," said the sick swallow. "I'm lovely and warm now. I shall soon get back my strength and be able to fly again, out in the warm sunshine."

"Ah, but it's so cold out of doors," she said. "It's snowing and freezing. Stay in your warm bed; I'll look after you all right."

Then she brought the swallow some water, in the petal of a flower, and the bird drank it and told her how it had torn one of its wings on a bramble and therefore couldn't fly as fast as the other swallows when they flew far, far away to the warm countries. At last it had fallen to the ground, but it couldn't remember anything after that and had no idea how it came to be where it was.

The swallow now remained here all through the winter, and Thumbelina took care of it and grew very fond of it. Neither the mole nor the field-mouse heard anything at all about this; they had no liking for the poor wretched swallow.

As soon as spring had arrived and the sun had begun to warm the earth, the swallow said goodbye to Thumbelina, who opened up the hole that the mole had made in the roof of the passage. The sun came shining in so pleasantly, and the swallow asked if she would like to come too; she could sit on its back, and they would fly far out into the green forest. But Thumbelina knew that it would grieve the old field-mouse, if she left her like that.

"No, I can't," said Thumbelina. "Goodbye goodbye, you dear kind girl," said the swallow, as it flew into the open sunshine. Thumbelina gazed after it with tears in her eyes, for she was so fond of the poor swallow.

"Tweet-tweet!" sang the bird and flew off to the woods...

Thumbelina felt so sad. She was never allowed to go out into the warm sunshine. The corn that had been sown in the field above the fieldmouse's home was certainly very tall; so that it was like a dense wood for the poor little girl, who after all was only an inch high.

"You will have to start making your wedding trousseau this summer," the field-mouse told her, because by now their neighbour, the tiresome tedious mole in the black velvet coat, had proposed to her. "You'll need to have both woollens and linen – something for every occasion – when you're married to the mole."

So Thumbelina had to spin from a distaff, and the field-mouse engaged four spiders to spin and weave day and night. Every evening there was a visit from the mole, who always kept on about how, when summer was over, the sun wasn't nearly so warm, whereas now it scorched the earth till it was as hard as a stone. Yes, and when the summer had ended there was to be his wedding with Thumbelina. But she wasn't at all pleased, for she found the mole such a terrible bore. Every morning, as the sun rose, and every evening as it set, she stole out to the door, and when the wind parted the ears of corn so that she could see the blue sky, she thought how lovely and bright it was out there and did so wish she could catch sight of the dear swallow once more; but the bird never came again and had evidently flown far off into the beautiful green forest.

Now it was autumn, and Thumbelina had the whole of her trousseau ready.

"Your wedding will be in four weeks' time," the field-mouse told her. But Thumbelina wept and said she wouldn't marry the tedious mole.

"Hoity-toity!" said the field-mouse. "Don't you be so pig-headed, or I'll bite you with my white teeth. Why, he's a splen-did husband for you. The Queen herself hasn't anything like his black velvet coat. His kitchen and cellar are both of the best. You ought to thank Heaven he's yours."

The wedding-day arrived. The mole was already there to fetch Thumbelina. She would have to live with him deep down under the earth and never come out into the warm sunshine, for he didn't care for that. The poor child was very sad at hav-ing to say goodbye to the beautiful sun, which she had at least been allowed to look at from the doorway when she was living with the field-mouse.

"Goodbye, bright sun!" she said and, stretching out her arms to it, she also took a few steps out from the field-mouse's dwelling; for the harvest was in, and nothing was left but the dry stubble. "Goodbye, goodbye," she said, throwing her tiny arms round a little red flower standing near. "Remember me to the dear swallow, if you happen to see it."

"Tweet-tweet!" she heard suddenly over her head. She looked up, and there was the swallow just passing. How delighted it was to see Thumbelina! She told the bird how she disliked having to marry the ugly mole and to live deep down under the earth where the sun never shone. She couldn't help crying at the thought.

"The cold winter will soon be here," said the swallow. "I'm going far away to the warm countries. Will you come with me? You can sit on my back. Just tie yourself on with your sash, and away we'll fly from the ugly mole and his dingy house, far away across the mountains, to the warm countries, where the sun shines more brightly than it does here and there's always summer with its lovely flowers. Dear little Thumbelina, do come with me – you who saved my life when I lay frozen stiff in that dismal cellar."

"Yes, I'll come with you," said Thumbelina. She climbed on to the bird's back, setting her feet on its outstretched wings and tying her sash to one of the strongest feathers. Then the swallow flew high up into the air, over lake and forest, high up over the great mountains of eternal snow. Thumbelina shivered in the cold air, but then she snuggled in under the bird's warm feathers, merely poking out her little head to look at all the loveliness stretched out beneath her.

And at last they reached the warm countries. The sun was shining there much more brightly than with us, and the sky looked twice as far off. On walls and slopes grew the finest black and white grapes, in the woods hung lemons and oranges; the air smelt sweetly of myrtle and curled mint, and the most delightful children darted about on the roads playing with large gay-coloured butterflies. But the swallow kept flying on and on, and the country became more and more beautiful, till at last they came upon an ancient palace of glittering white marble standing among vivid green trees beside a blue lake. Vines went curling up round the tall pillars, and right at the top were a number of swallow's nests. One of these was the home of the swallow that had brought Thumbelina on its back.

"Here's my house," cried the swallow.

"But you see those beautiful flowers growing down here? You shall now choose one of them yourself, and then I'll put you on it, and you can make yourself as cosy as you like."

"That will be lovely," she said, clapping her little hands.

A large white marble column was lying there on the ground just as it had fallen and broken into three pieces, but in among these were growing the most beautiful white flowers. The swallow flew down with Thumbelina and placed her on one of the broad petals – but what a surprise she got! There in the middle of the flower sat a little man as white and transparent as if he had been made of glass. He wore the neatest little gold crown on his head and the most exquisite wings on his shoulders; he himself was no bigger than Thumbelina. He was the guardian spirit of the flower. Each flower had just such a little man or woman living in it, but this one was King of them all.

"Goodness, how handsome he is!" whispered Thumbelina to the swallow. The little monarch was very frightened of the swallow, which of course seemed a gigantic bird beside one so small and delicate as himself; but when he caught sight of Thumbelina he was enchanted, for she was much the prettiest little lady he had ever seen. So he took the gold crown off his head and placed it on hers. At the same time he asked her what her name was and whether she would be his wife; if so, she would become Queen of all the flowers. Well, he would be a proper husband for her, quite different from the son of the old toad and from the mole with the black velvet coat. So she said yes to the handsome King, and from every flower there appeared a lady or a gentleman that was the most dapper little creature imaginable. Each one brought a present for Thumbelina, but the best of them all was a pair of beautiful wings from a large white fly. These were fastened to her back, so that she too could flit from flower to flower. There was such rejoicing, and the swallow sat up above in its nest and sang for them as well as it could, but the poor bird was really too sad at heart, for it was very fond of Thumbelina and would have liked never to be parted from her.

"You shan't be called Thumbelina," said the guardian spirit of the flower to her. "It's an ugly name, and you are so pretty. We will call you Maia."

"Goodbye, goodbye," said the swallow and flew away again from the warm countries, far away back to Denmark. There it had a little nest above the window where the man lives who can tell fairy tales, and there it was that the swallow sang "Tweet-tweet!" to him... And that's where the whole story comes from.

SIMPLE SIMON

(A NURSERY TALE RETOLD)

Away in the country, in an old manorhouse, lived an old squire. He had two sons who were so clever that – well, the fact is they were too clever by half. They made up their minds to go and propose to the King's daughter; and they had a perfect right to do this, because she had announced that she would marry the man who she thought was best able to speak up for himself.

The two sons now spent a week in preparation. A week was all they were allowed; but it was quite long enough, for they had had a good education, and that is such a help. One of them knew the whole Latin dictionary off by heart, and also the local newspaper for the last three years, both backwards and forwards. The other son had learnt up all the by-laws of the city companies and the things every alderman is supposed to know; he thought this would help him to talk politics with the Princess; and, besides, he knew how to embroider braces, he was so very clever with his fingers.

"I shall win the Princess!" cried both of them; and so their father gave them each a beautiful horse. The brother who had learnt off the dictionary and the newspapers got a coal-black horse; and the one who knew all about aldermen and could do embroidery got a milk-white horse; and then they smeared the corners of their mouths with cod-liver oil, so that the words would come out pat. All the servants were down in the courtyard to see them mount their horses, when just at that moment up came the third brother; for there were three of them, though nobody ever took count of the third, because he wasn't a scholar like the other two. They called him Simple Simon.

"Where are you two off to in that get up?" he asked.

"We're going to Court, to talk our way into favour with the Princess. Haven't you heard the proclamation that's been read out all over the country?" And then they told him all about it.

"Gosh! I mustn't miss this!" said Simple Simon. But his brothers laughed at him and rode away.

"Dad, let me have a horse!" cried Simple Simon. "I do so feel like getting married. If she'll have me, she'll have me; and if she won't, then I'll marry her all the same."

"What nonsense!" said the father. "I've no horse for you. Why, you never open your mouth. But look at your brothers – they are splendid fellows."

"If I can't have a horse," said the boy, "then I'll ride the billy-goat. It's my own, and it'll carry me all right, I know." Then he got astride the billy-goat, dug his heels into its sides and dashed off down the road. Phew! What a rate they went! "Look out! Here we come!" yelled Simple Simon, and his cries went echoing after him.

But his brothers rode on ahead in complete silence. They never said a word, because they had to turn over in their minds all the clever remarks they were going to make. It had to be most cunningly worked out, I can tell you.

"Tally-ho!" shouted Simple Simon, "here we are! Look what I found on the road," and he showed them a dead crow he had picked up.

"You simpleton!" they said. "What are you going to do with that?"

"I shall give it to the Princess."

"Yes, do!" they answered, laughing as they rode on.

"Tally-ho! Here we are! Now look what I've found. You don't find that on the road every day."

The brothers turned round again to see what it was. "You simpleton!" they said. "Why, that's an old clog with the vamp missing. Is the Princess to have that as well?"

"Yes, of course," said Simple Simon; and his brothers only laughed at him and rode on till they were a long way ahead.

"Tally-ho! Here we are!" shouted Simon. "My word! This is getting better and better. Tally-ho! This is grand!"

"What have you found this time?" asked the brothers.

"Oh, it's too good for anything," said Simple Simon. "Won't she be pleased, the Princess!"

"Ugh!" said the brothers. "Why, it's mud straight out of the ditch."

"Yes, that's just what it is," said Simple Simon, "and the very finest sort, too; it slips right through your fingers." And he filled his pocket with the mud.

But his two brothers rode on as hard as they could go, and the result was that they drew up at the city gate a whole hour ahead of him and found the suitors being given numbers in the order of their arrival. They were made to stand in rows, six in each file, and so close together that they couldn't move their arms. This was just as well, for otherwise they might have stabbed each other in the back, just because one was in front of the other.

The rest of the inhabitants all crowded round the castle,

right up against the windows, so as to watch the Princess receiving her suitors; but as soon as ever one of them came into her presence, he was completely tongue-tied. "No good!" the Princess kept saying. "Skedaddle!"

Now it was the turn of the brother who knew the dictionary by heart. But he had clean forgotten it while he was standing in the queue; and the floor creaked under him, and the ceiling was all covered with mirrors, so that he saw himself standing on his head. At the window stood three clerks and an alderman, who all wrote down every word that was spoken, so that it could go straight into the newspaper and be sold for a penny at the street-corner. It was dreadful; and what's more, they had made up such a fire that the stove was red-hot.

"It's very warm in here," said the suitor.

"That's because my father's roasting cockerels today," said the Princess.

"O-o-oh!" was all he could say, as he stood there. He hadn't expected a remark like that, and he was hoping to say something witty. "O-o-oh!"

"No good!" said the Princess. "Skedaddle!" – and away he had to go. After that the second brother came in.

"It's dreadfully hot in here," he said.

"Yes, we're roasting cockerels for dinner," said the Princess.

"I b-beg your – b-beg your -" he stuttered; and the clerks all wrote down "I b-beg your – b-beg your -"

"No good!" said the Princess. "Skedaddle!"

Now it was Simple Simon's turn. He came trotting in on the billygoat, right into the palace-room. "Why, it's as hot as blazes in here!" he said.

"That's because I'm roasting cockerels," said the Princess.

"Oh, I say, that's lucky," said Simple Simon. "So I suppose I can have a crow roasted, can't I!"

"Of course you can, quite easily," said the Princess; "but have you got anything to roast it in, for I've neither pot nor pan."

"But I have," said Simon. "Here's a cooker with a tin handle!" And he produced the old clog and popped the crow straight into it.

"It will make quite a meal," said the Princess. "But what shall we do for gravy?"

"I've got that in my pocket," said Simon. "I've enough and to spare." And he tipped a little mud out of his pocket.

"I do like that!" said the Princess. "You know how to answer; you can speak up for yourself, and you're the one I'm going to marry! But do you realize that every word we've been saying has been written down and will be in the papers to-morrow? Look there by the window – three clerks and an old alderman; and the alderman is the worst, because he doesn't understand a thing." Of course she said this just to frighten him. And the clerks all guffawed and made a great blot of ink on the floor.

"So these are the gentry?" said Simon. "Well, here's one for the alderman!" And he turned out his pocket and let him have the mud full in the face.

"Well done!" cried the Princess. "I could never have done that, but I'll soon learn." So in the end Simple Simon became King with a wife of his own and a crown and a throne. And all this comes straight out of the alderman's newspaper; so it may not be perfectly true!

THE TOP AND THE BALL

A top and a ball were in a drawer together with some other toys, and then one day the top said to the ball: "Look here, we live together in the same drawer – shall we become engaged?" But the ball, who was made of morocco leather and fancied herself quite as much as any smart young lady, wouldn't even answer such a ridiculous question.

Next day the little boy whom the toys belonged to came and painted the top red and yellow all over and hammered a brass nail into the middle of it. The top was really a fine sight, as it went spinning round and round.

"Look at me!" said the top to the ball. "What do you say now? Don't you think after all we might be engaged? We go so splendidly together: you bounce and I dance. There couldn't be a happier couple than us two."

"Oh, you think that, do you?" answered the ball. "You don't seem to realize that my father and mother were morocco slippers and that I have a cork inside me."

"Ah, but I'm made of mahogany," said the top. "Why, the mayor turned me himself on his own lathe, and he was so pleased about it."

"Am I really expected to believe that?" asked the ball.

"May I never be whipped again, if I'm not telling you the truth!" answered the top.

"You give a very fine account of yourself," said the ball. "But I really must say no. You see, I'm what you might call half-engaged to a swallow. Every time I go up in the air, he pops his head out of the nest and says: "Will you? Will you?" I've already said to myself that I will, and that's as good as a half-engagement. But I promise never to forget you."

"A lot of good that'll be!" replied the top; and they said no more to each other.

Next day the ball was taken out into the garden. The top watched how she flew high up into the air, just like a bird, until she went clean out of sight. But she came back again each time and, whether from longing or because she had a cork inside her, this was always followed by a high bounce as soon as she touched the ground. The ninth time the ball went up, she never came back; the little boy looked and looked, but she had vanished.

"Ah, I could tell him where she is," said the top with a sigh. "She's in the swallow's nest and has married the swallow."

The more the top thought it all over, the more he lost his heart to the ball. The mere fact that he couldn't have her made him love her more than ever; the strange thing was that she should have accepted anyone else.

And the top went on dancing and spinning round, but all the time he was thinking about the ball, who grew more and more beautiful in his imagination. In this way several years went by, till gradually it became nothing more than an old love-affair...

But, although the top was no longer young, suddenly one day he found himself painted all over with gold. Never had he looked so handsome; he was now a gold top, and he whirled and whirled until he hummed. Gosh! It was something like! Then all at once he jumped too high – and disappeared. They looked and looked, even down in the basement, but he was not to be found.

Wherever had he got to?

He had jumped into the dustbin among all sorts of cabbage-stalks, sweepings and rubbish that had come down from the gutter on the roof.

"Here's a nice place for me to come to!" said the top. "My gold paint will soon go off and – did you ever see such riff-raff as I've got around me!" And then he peeped sideways at a long skinny-looking cabbagestalk and a curious round object that looked like an old apple... But it wasn't an apple at all, it was an old ball that had been lying up in the gutter on the roof for several years and become quite sodden.

"Thank goodness, here's someone at last of one's own class that one can talk to," said the ball, with a glance at the gilded top, "Actually I'm made of morocco leather, stitched by gentlewomen, and I've got a cork inside me, but nobody would ever think so to look at me. I was just going to marry a swallow, when I landed up in the gutter; and there I've been for five years growing more and more sodden. That's a long time, believe me, for a young lady."

But the top didn't say a word. His thoughts went back to his old sweetheart, and the longer he listened the more certain he became that this was her.

Presently the maidservant came to clear out the dustbin. "Well, I never! Here's the gold top!" she said. Back in the house the top came in for lots of attention, but nothing was said about the ball, and the top never spoke again of his old love.

Love is, of course, bound to fade away, when your sweetheart has spent five years growing sodden in a gutter; you can't be expected to know her again, if you meet her in a dustbin.